Words to Know Before You Read

ashamed

blurted

embarrassed

explored

fascinating

gigantic

nervous

shun

www.rourkepublishing.com

Edited by Luana K. Mitten
Illustrated by Helen Poole
Art Direction and Page Layout by Renee Brady

Library of Congress Cataloging-in-Publication Data

Steinkraus, Kyla
 Fish Stories / Kyla Steinkraus.
     p. cm. -- (Little Birdie Books)
 ISBN 978-1-61741-831-0 (hard cover) (alk. paper)
 ISBN 978-1-61236-035-5 (soft cover)
 Library of Congress Control Number: 2011924715

Rourke Publishing
Printed in the United States of America, North Mankato, Minnesota
060711
060711CL

www.rourkepublishing.com - rourke@rourkepublishing.com
Post Office Box 643328 Vero Beach, Florida 32964

Fish Stories

By Kyla Steinkraus

Illustrated by Helen Poole

It was the first day of second grade, and Scott was excited to see his friends after a long summer. The teacher asked all the students to tell a story about their summer vacation.

Cindy told the class how she explored castles in Europe. Michael went horseback riding and hiking in the mountains.

Summer Vacation

show and tell

Scott didn't have any fascinating stories to tell. He spent the summer with a babysitter while his parents worked. One Sunday, Dad took him fishing, but all he caught was a teeny, tiny minnow.

It was nearly his turn when Julie stood up. "We stayed in a cabin on a lake. I caught a fish as big as my lunch box!"

"Oh!" Cindy gushed.

"That's so cool!" added Michael.

"I went fishing too," Scott said quickly. "But my fish was gigantic. It was as big as . . . as big as my desk!"

"Oh, wow!" said Julie. "Did you take a picture?"

10

"Of course," Scott replied, and before he knew it, he had promised to bring a picture to school the next day.

Scott felt horrible. His heart felt like it was being squeezed tighter and tighter. What was he going to do? He had lied. He didn't have a picture of the fish he hadn't caught.

When they found out, his friends wouldn't want to be his friends anymore. They would laugh at him. They would shun him.

At recess, Cindy offered to push him on the swing. Scott shook his head and sat by himself.

At lunch, Michael asked Scott to sit with him. Scott was afraid Michael would ask him questions about the gigantic fish, so Scott sat at an empty table instead.

After school, Scott's friends walked up to him. "Are you okay?" Julie asked.

"You've been acting weird all day," Michael said.

Scott's face reddened. He felt embarrassed and scared. But he also hated feeling ashamed and nervous around his friends.

"I lied," he blurted. "I only caught a small minnow, but I wanted to have a cool story to tell."

Cindy hugged him. "That's okay."

"You aren't mad?" Scott asked.

Michael patted his shoulder. "Friends forgive each other."

"You told us the truth," Julie said. "I bet that was hard to do."

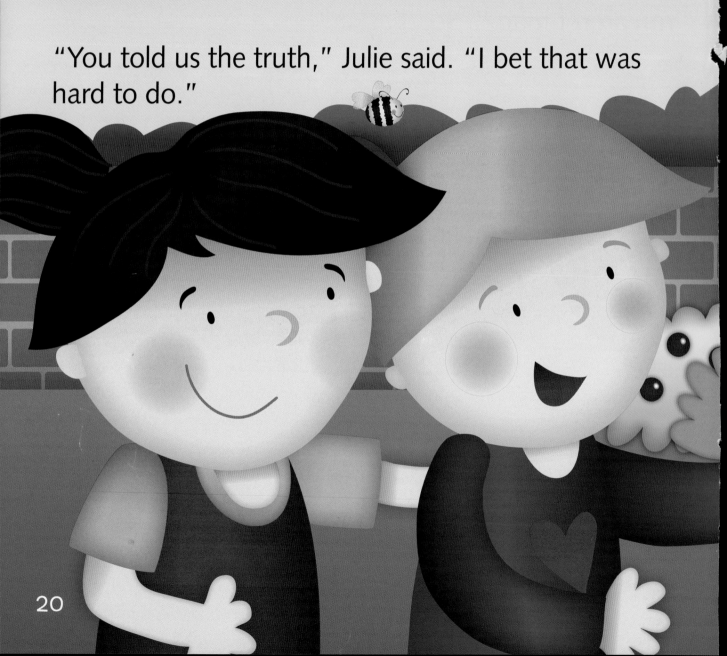

"It sure was," Scott said, smiling. Suddenly he felt as light as a feather! "I think the second day of second grade is going to be a much better day!"

After Reading Activities

You and the Story...

Why did Scott tell a lie?

How did telling a lie make Scott feel?

What do you think would've happened if Scott didn't tell his friends the truth?

Think of a time you've told a lie. How did it make you feel?

Words You Know Now...

Some of the words below have endings. On a piece of paper write each word below. If it has an ending, write the word without the ending. Does the meaning change without the ending?

ashamed	fascinating
blurted	gigantic
embarrassed	nervous
explored	shun

- Where would you like to go on vacation?

- Read about where you want to go. What are some fun things you could do on your vacation?

- Who is going with you?

- When would you like to go?

- Make a list of everything you will need to take on your vacation.

About the Author

Kyla Steinkraus lives in Tampa, Florida with her husband and two kids. She tried fishing several times, but she didn't catch anything, not even a minnow!

About the Illustrator

Helen Poole lives in Liverpool, England, with her fiancé. Over the past ten years she has worked as a Designer and Illustrator on books, toys, and games for many stores and publishers worldwide. Her favorite part of illustrating is character development. She loves creating fun, whimsical worlds with

bright, vibrant colors. She gets her inspiration from everyday life and has her sketchbook with her at all times as inspiration often strikes in the unlikeliest of places!